2.50

D0426925

LITTLE KING
DECEMBER

LITTLE KING DECEMBER

Axel Hacke

Illustrated by Michael Sowa

Translated from the German
by Rosemary Davidson

BLOOMSBURY

For Ursula

F or some time I've been getting visits, every now and again, from December II, the little pot-bellied king. He's about three inches tall, and so fat that he can't button up his tiny red velvet coat with its magnificent ermine trim.

The little king adores jelly bears. To eat them he has to hug them with both arms, only just managing to lift them up, because each is about half his size. The little king sinks his teeth into the soft jelly bear, taking big bites out of it, and asks the same thing he asks me every time:

'Will you tell me about your country?'

The first time he came, I told him:

'Where I come from, you are born little, then you get bigger and bigger, sometimes almost as big as a basketball player. Once you stop growing, you start getting a little bit smaller again. Until finally you die, and disappear.'

'But that doesn't make sense,' said the little king, biting off his jelly bear's right paw. 'You should start out big, then get smaller and smaller and finally disappear – simply because you become so tiny you are invisible.'

'I think the Guild of Funeral Directors might have a problem with that,' I say to him.

'But that's how it is where I come from. My father, King December I, got so little that one morning his servant couldn't find him anywhere in his bed. That very same day, I was crowned king.'

'All right – but how can you be born big?' I ask. 'Everyone must come out of their mummy's tummy! And a mummy can't be smaller than her own baby!'

'Their mummy's tummy!' exclaimed December. 'Well I never! Me, one morning I woke up in my bed and went to work at the princes' office. That's all there is to it. Their mummy's tummy! Absolute nonsense! You wake up, and off you go!'

'And how exactly do you get to be in the bed?'

'Wait a minute,' said the king. 'I think . . . um . . . a king . . . a queen . . . well . . . what happens again? . . . Oh, I don't know! I'm already very small, you know. I've forgotten. I only remember that it's awfully nice.' He gave a little chuckle and bit once more into his jelly bear.

I said to him: 'Here, when a child is born, it knows nothing. It has to learn to eat and to walk, to read and to write. You wipe its nose clean, and by playing Ludo it learns not to be unbearable. It always has grown-ups to guide it, to turn its head from one side to the other, to lift its chin . . .'

The king burped loudly and was briefly convulsed with laughter. In the meantime, he had swallowed his jelly bear's head.

Chewing, he looked at me steadily and cried: 'And then?'

'Then, you get big,' I replied.

'Does it hurt?'

'It happens very slowly. Well, that said, some children grow two centimetres in a single night, and if you put your ear to their arms and legs you can hear them creak.'

'It's the same for us, except it's the other way round,' December declared. 'You notice that you've got smaller only every now and again. Like the other day: in the evening I could still put my teacup on the table, and the next morning I had to climb up on to a chair to reach it. Is it good to get bigger, do you think?'

'Until now, it hadn't occurred to me that there was an alternative.'

'But now you know,' he said.

'Tell me a bit more,' I asked. 'What do you know already when you are born and what do you learn later?'

'Almost everything,' announced the little pot-bellied king. 'You wake up, you lie there for a bit, you get up and you can write, do higher mathematics, write computer programs, you go to work and to business dinners. No problem! Only gradually you forget. The smaller you get, the more you forget. If someone can no longer participate in business dinners, it's pointless going to the office: there's no need for them there any more. Then you have to stay at home and you carry on forgetting more and more things. Your head becomes completely empty, with lots of room. Others have to cook for you, and afterwards you're allowed to go and see your friends. Or watch shadows in the garden and pretend they're ghosts. Or give names to the clouds. Or torture your teddy bear.

Or . . .'

I interrupted: 'Unless the grown-ups tell you not to.'

'It's got nothing to do with the grown-ups!' retorted the king. 'The smaller you are, the more authority you have, because . . . because you have more experience of life. Ho ho! And the grown-ups have to answer all your questions: Why does a house have corners? Why are there only six numbers on a dice? Why does it rain? As soon as you have the answer, it's your prerogative to forget it immediately. And because the little ones are in charge, our escalators all have tiny steps, and our toilets are minute so we can't fall into them. While you're still big, it's not so good, but that's how it is.'

He stood up with a quick, proud movement, put what was left of his jelly bear on the floor and set about buttoning up his coat. An impossibility, because his stomach is so-o-o-o-o big. He sat down again with a sigh.

'If I understand it,' I said, putting his jelly bear back in his hands, 'where you come from, childhood happens at the end of life?'

'Of course!' the king replied. 'Think about it: that way you have something to look forward to!' He looked at me for a long time. 'Do you know what I think?'

'No.'

'I think it's not that you really get bigger. It just seems that you do.'

'What do you mean?'

'I think that you start out big too. Well, that is if what you're telling me is true . . . This is how I see things: you start out with everything at the beginning; and each day, something is taken away from you. You have a lot of imagination when you are small, but really you know very little. As a result, you have to think about things all the time: How does the light get into the lamp, and the image into the television? Why do dwarves live under the roots of trees, and what is it like to find yourself standing in the palm of a giant's hand? Then, you grow up, and those who are bigger than you explain to you how the light and the television work. Then, you learn that there are neither dwarves nor giants. Your imagination shrinks as your knowledge grows. Am I wrong?'

'No,' I whispered, then added, even quieter still, 'but it's not so bad to grow up, to learn, to understand the world, to . . .'

He continued: 'You get old. At first, you want to be a fireman or something, a nurse or whatever. And one day you are a nurse or a fireman and not something else. It's too late to change your mind. That too in a way is to grow smaller, isn't it?'

'Oh yes. Yes!' I say with a sigh.

'It's so much better for us,' continued the little pot-bellied king, taking a last bite out of his jelly bear. 'I feel sorry for you; well, for all of you, of course.'

He got up, squeezed his tummy through the gap between my bookshelf and the wall and, as is his wont, disappeared once again from the room without saying goodbye, just a tiny bit smaller.

There was a time when I was often sad, so sad that at night when it was dark I would walk through the town alone, and I was happy when it rained. Outside in the streets everything was dark and wet, and my sadness was reflected in the puddles and this reflection was a comfort to me. I no longer felt so alone.

When I had walked enough, I'd climb back up the old wooden staircase to my apartment and sit down in a chair. On one of those evenings, King December II appeared out of the little gap between the bookcase and the wall and said to me:

'Where were you?'

'Oh, don't ask . . .'

'And how are you?'

'Oh, you know . . .'

'What are you going to do now?'

'Sleep.'

'Come to my house for a bit,' King December suggested.

'How am I supposed to do that? You live behind a shelf, and

the only way in is through a tiny hole. I'm much too big to get through it, even at this time of night.'

For it so happens that at night I am five centimetres smaller than in the morning, when I have been stretched and lengthened by sleep. In the evening, life has crushed me. But not small enough to visit King December behind his little crack in the wall, I thought.

'You've never tried,' protested the king. 'Get down on your stomach in front of my apartment and you'll see.'

I lay down on my stomach. The parquet creaked and the king disappeared through his hole.

'Now stick your two index fingers into the chink,' he shouted from inside, 'and pull yourself slowly in towards me.'

I put my two fingers into the opening, just as he said, gripped the wall on each side and pulled myself forwards. The bookshelf creaked. I noticed a huge dustball and thought to myself that I should do some cleaning – the dustballs were almost as big as my head. Suddenly, my head was in, and then the rest of me followed.

I found myself flat on my stomach in the king's apartment.

'Heavens above! I would never have believed it!' I cried.

I stood up. The king was now a little taller than me, but even for someone so tiny, his apartment was extraordinarily small. It was just one room, and in five strides he could get from one end of it to the other.

'Is this it?' I asked him. 'I mean, is this the whole apartment?'

'Alas, yes,' he sighed. 'The house is a hundred years old; it's very tired, and it gets smaller and smaller every year. Houses also get smaller when they are tired, but not many people know that. Fifty years ago this room was eight times as big as it is now.' He was quiet for a second, sighed, then added:

'Me too, alas.'

I looked around. To the left of the entrance the king had a little narrow bed with pillows covered in a beautiful deep-red silk which glimmered in the light of the candle on his bedside table. There was no other furniture, not even a chair. But the walls were covered in dark wooden shelves that were filled with boxes,

hundreds of little boxes, a bit like the ones that rings come in from jewellers. They were all sorts of colours, and each had a different decoration: a snake, flowers, a house or a little car, trains and people, or even dragons and pointy-hatted fairies.

'What do you keep in these boxes?' I asked.

'My dreams,' said King December.

'Your dreams!?'

'All my dreams. One dream per box.'

'But how do you dream your dreams if you close them up in boxes?'

'In the evening when I'm going to sleep,' said the king, 'I take a box from the shelves, put it by my bed and take the lid off. Then I go to sleep and I dream. In the morning when I wake up I stay in bed for a bit and think about the night. Then I put the dream back in its box and put it back on the shelf. What did you dream about last night?' he asked.

'Oh, I can't really remember,' I said. 'I . . . I was sitting in a boat, I think, and I was rowing on a dark and peaceful lake. But I was getting nowhere and while I rowed I looked through a window which was level with my face the whole time – a window in a rowing boat, funny that, don't you think? But I didn't find it funny at all, because the whole time I was feeling sad because I could only row so slowly. Through the window I looked out on to a black lake, on which I saw myself sitting in a rowing boat looking through a window at myself rowing, and so on and so on.'

'And what happened?' asked the little pot-bellied king. He had been sitting on the edge of the bed the whole time, looking at me and breathing softly.

'Nothing happened,' I said. 'I rowed and I looked at myself rowing in the window, looking at myself rowing, and so on, over and over to infinity.'

'Ho ho ho!' cried the king. 'That's a dream for a ve-r-r-r-y big box!'

'Where do they come from, your boxes? Are they all full? And have you dreamed everything that's in them?'

'Oh, no! Not at all,' said the king. 'I inherited them from my grandfather, King January III. He lived in a room like this one – we all live in rooms like this one. His room was in a very old house. He was getting older and older, and smaller and smaller, and so was the house and so was the room. Only the boxes stayed the same size, because dreams always stay big and need room. So my grandfather lived in his room, and the older he got, the more space the boxes took up and the more his dreams crowded in on him in the ever-shrinking room, until one day the room got so small that the boxes filled it entirely. Grandfather himself had become so minute by this time that you couldn't see him any more. He was so tiny among the giant dreams that it was impossible to find him, and he got lost among them. In the end I moved the boxes to a bigger room: this one that we're in now. Now they are mine. But – who knows? – perhaps my grandfather is still here among them somewhere.'

The king was sitting on the edge of his bed, his legs swinging, his eyes twinkling in the candlelight.

'The older we get, the more powerful our dreams become,' I said softly, 'until we live only through them, scrambling from box to box and wandering through huge giant-size images. And it's the same for you.'

'The same,' he replied.

'The same,' I sighed. 'Do you know which dream is in which box?'

'What do you think this is — a video store?' exclaimed December, raising his voice. 'I mean, you can't just choose which dream you want to dream — one day one about princesses, the next one about cowboys . . . Of course I don't know which dream is in which box. It's a surprise. You can't choose.'

He took off his little red velvet coat, hung it on a gold hook on one of the shelves and neatly placed his beautiful golden shoes at the foot of his bed. Then he got into bed, his crown on his head. But he'd scarcely lain down before he got up and started walking up and down the room, barefoot in his little white shirt.

'Tell me another dream!' he said.

'Not long ago I dreamed I was a fighter pilot. But I never flew in my plane — I just drove about in it. I drove along the motorway and country roads and when I came to the town I parked it in a car park just beside the city wall, got a ticket from the parking machine and went to see my best friend. While we were having a coffee my friend asked me where my plane was.

"In the car park in front of the house," I said. "You can't leave a fighter plane in a car park. A fighter plane belongs on an airfield or in the air." I went outside to drive my plane to an airfield. Then I realised that I couldn't drive it on the road any more, I had to fly it. But how do you take off in a fighter plane in the middle of a town? That wasn't going to work either. So I sat there

in my plane like an idiot. I was in despair – I had no idea what to do: a pilot who can't fly and who doesn't dare to move his fighter plane.'

'You poor thing!' said the king, deep in thought. 'Even in your dream you can't take off. You really make me sad. No wonder you're unhappy.'

'At least if I was still small,' I said, 'I might still become a pilot one day.'

'I think I'll be one, one day,' said the king. 'A pilot, I mean.' His eyes wandered over the countless boxes all around us, and he said, 'I'll definitely be a pilot. When I'm really little, I'll be a pilot. Anyway, I'll dream of being one. Somewhere in these boxes there's a big, long pilot dream, and I'm definitely going to find it.'

'You're lucky,' I said.

'Do you know what?' said King December.

'No, what?'

'I think that you didn't dream that you were a pilot. You really were one.'

'Really . . .' I said.

'Imagine,' he continued. 'You really are a pilot who doesn't know how to fly, and another day you are a sad, rowing man, and then another day you are . . . oh, I don't know. That's the way life is. Life begins at night, when you go to sleep, and goes on hold in the morning when you wake up. You just need to say "wake up" instead of "go to sleep" and "go to sleep" instead of "wake up". What's your job?'

'I'm someone who goes to an office.'

'Aha,' said the king. 'So, you go to sleep, in the morning and dream all day that you are at the office and that you work, work, work. And at night, as soon as you've gone to bed, you wake up and all night you are what you really are. Sometimes a pilot, sometimes a rower, and sometimes an I-don't-know-what. Don't you think it's better that way round?'

'I don't know. How is that better?' I said.

'It's more varied,' the king explained. 'And the night becomes more important. The day is just a dream, and everything that happens during the day is no longer such a big deal.'

'Do you think so?' I said.

'You came to me here awake,' said the king. 'And you are still awake. But you are lying in a little room with a tiny little king, and you are tinier still. That can't be real. Or can it?'

'Can you prove it's real?' I asked.

'Well really,' said King December, 'kings like me don't exist.'

'Are you dreaming at the moment then, or are you awake?' I asked.

The king smiled and said, 'You are dreaming me and I am dreaming you.'

'Or the other way round,' I said.

'Yes,' said the king.

'Yet, you are awake. You're not sleeping.'

'How do you know?' he asked.

'It's all so complicated,' I groaned.

'Disconcerting. But not complicated,' he corrected.

All this time he had been pacing up and down the room, but now he stood still, the little pot-bellied king, and stared down at me long and hard. Down at me because I was still lying on the floor. I held his gaze for a long time, until my eyes grew tired and I closed them. I fell asleep on the floor of the little room, and the last thing I remember was the little box on King December's bedside table; a bright-red box decorated with shining gold crowns, open, its lid lying beside it. The whole time, I hadn't even noticed it.

L ittle King December is an early bird. Often in the morning when I go to sit down for my breakfast he's already there, sitting on the headline of the newspaper, covering up exactly three letters, so that instead of 'Prime Minister' I read 'Prime Minis', and then I see the small, fat king. But mostly he sits in the bread-basket, warming himself near the toast. I think it must be pretty cold behind the bookshelf, even if you're wearing a thick velvet robe.

'Get away from the toast,' I scolded recently, 'or I'll eat you by mistake.'

'I am so bored,' he said. I thought he had got quite a bit smaller since I'd first set eyes on him. Now he was only a tiny bit taller than my little finger.

'Eat a jelly bear then,' I said.

'I've just had one.'

'You could climb around in the books.'

'I've already done that.'

'Then tidy up your boxes of dreams.'

'I've done that too.'

'Well, in that case I don't know what to suggest.'

'I don't know what to do.'

'I want to have my breakfast in peace.'

'You never take me anywhere.'

'Where am I supposed to take you?'

'I don't know. I've never been out. How should I know whether it's beautiful outside, and whether that's where I want to be? Where do you go everyday after breakfast?'

'To the office,' I said. 'I go down Cornelius Street to Garden Square, then across Flower Street and Jacob Square to Post Street. I make that trip every day, and every evening I come home – always by the same route and from the same office.'

'And what do you do at the office?' he asked.

'I occupy myself with reality,' I said. 'Most people who sit all day in offices occupy themselves with reality.'

'Take me with you,' said the king.

'Today's my day off,' I said. 'So I'm staying at home.'

'Let's go anyway!' cried the king.

'What would I do at the office on my day off?' I asked.

'Is there no reality today?' asked the king.

'Yes,' I said. 'But my colleagues are dealing with it. I'm going to relax, so that I feel fresh for tomorrow.'

'So today you have a reality-free day!' cried the king, and thumped his fist so enthusiastically on the rim of my plate that the fork rattled. 'Hey, we don't have to go to the office. We can turn back before we get there. But you could at least show me the way!'

'It's such a boring journey!' I groaned. 'Every day the same route, and then you expect me to go on my day off too?!'

'It's so dull around here!' shouted the king. He kicked angrily at the toast on my plate, sending crumbs flying. Then he started stabbing little holes in the butter with his sceptre. Finally, panting with the effort, he started lifting sugar cubes high above his head, throwing them with all his might, one after the other, into my coffee.

'Stop that at once!' I yelled.

'I am King December II!' he shouted. 'And you are not a king. You must do what I say.'

'All right, then. I can't drink my coffee now anyway, with all that sugar in it. But we're not going to my office. We'll turn around before we get there and come back.'

'Well, that's what I said!' he cried happily.

I put on a jacket, took the little king and put him in my top pocket like a handkerchief so that his head and crown peeked out and he could look around.

'If someone's coming,' I said, 'you duck down inside, OK? I don't want anyone to see you.'

'I'll watch out,' he said, trembling with excitement.

So we went downstairs, opened the big heavy front door and went out into the street. It was a beautiful spring day. The Isar was flowing full and fast with yellow melt-water from the mountains, and the sun shone on our faces.

'Oh-h-h-h!' cried the little king. 'It's so-o-o beau-u-tiful!'

'Be quiet!' I hissed. We went left towards Cornelius Street. As we went along I quietly explained everything we saw to little King December. When we went past a tailor's I said, 'That's a tailor's shop,' and explained to him what a tailor did. When we saw a baker's, I said, 'That's a baker's,' and told him how a baker worked. If we went past a shop selling leather whips for men, I pointed over to the other side of the road and said, 'Look, there's a wallpaper shop,' and explained what wallpaper is. I really knew my way around; and each time the king would say something like, 'I knew that once,' or 'I'd completely forgotten that,' or 'Gosh, that was such a long time ago!'

Of course we also came across some people as we went. Most were people I saw every day on my way to work, who I knew vaguely but no longer paid the slightest attention to. The king, however, stared at each of them intently, and when I anxiously whispered to him that he should tuck himself down in my pocket like we agreed, or pushed him back in so roughly that his crown fell off, he would pop his head back up again immediately and make some comment about the people we saw.

For example, we passed the little old man who always walked a poodle on a lead, and the king said, 'He's going to try to kill him again.'

'What did you say?' I asked.

'He's going to try to kill the poodle again. Do you know that that old man has been married to the same woman for fifty-two years. They live in a little apartment and he loves potato dumplings in sauce. He's only allowed to smoke his cigarettes in the kitchen over the oven grate with the window open. His wife insists. And when he's filling in his lottery numbers his wife dictates them to him: their wedding anniversary, for example. And whenever he just wants to lie on the sofa in the living room in his dressing gown memorising the wallpaper pattern, his wife's best friend is sure to turn up. He'd much rather kill his wife, obviously, but he doesn't dare. And anyway, he doesn't know how to make potato dumplings. So each day he tries to kill the poodle. It's his wife's. He's thrown it into the Isar once already, but it climbed on to a branch that was being carried along and the fire brigade

rescued it near the pine forest. Another time he threw the poodle off the top of the tower of St Peter's church, and lo and behold it suddenly sprouted wings and fluttered to the ground, barking gaily. Recently he tied it up in the park in front of the Patent Office and left it there. But someone had just registered a patent for a poodle-saving machine, so it was child's play for them to bring the animal back home safely. But the old man doesn't give up – his hatred is great and there's nothing else he can do.'

I looked down at my jacket pocket in complete amazement.

'How do you know all that?' I asked.

'I don't know it at all,' said the king. He was about to say something else when he saw a man wearing dark glasses and a wide-brimmed hat and walking so close to the walls of the houses that his jacket was covered with stripes of white dust. He was looking around constantly, a worried expression on his face.

'That man is afraid of his neighbour,' said the king. 'She's in love with him and constantly pursues him. The minute she sees a light on in his apartment she's at the door. Once she even tried to break the door down. He opened it just at that moment and she went flying into the room and he took the chance to slip out past her into the street. Now he has to stay quiet as a mouse when he's at home, and since she can see from her apartment when there's a light on in his kitchen, he makes his dinner in the dark.'

'Why doesn't he move into another apartment?' I asked.

The king looked at me with disdain. 'Move? This is Munich, if I'm not mistaken?'

'Yes,' I replied, and the king said:

'Just because you're having a break from reality today, it doesn't mean you can forget the state of the property market.'

Just then an unshaven man with a greying crewcut came towards us. He was wearing a long white shirt and had sandals on his bare feet, and he was walking right in the middle of the road.

'It's the poet,' said the little king. 'He's calming the traffic.' The man had his arms outstretched, like a preacher blessing his congregation. The other passers-by paid no attention and went on their way without even looking at him. The cars on either side drove past slowly.

'The poet is a poet by night,' continued the king. 'In the morning he returns to the world for a couple of hours. He wants to get out and do something for others – that's why he's calming the traffic. Odd fellow, don't you think?'

'Very odd,' I said. 'But odder still is that I've never seen him before.'

'Well, you've never had me with you before. By the way, do you think there are dragons around here?'

'Dragons?' I said. 'Why would there be dragons? Listen, it's weird enough that there are little kings and poodle-saving machines and traffic-calming poets. You want there to be dragons as well? There are no dragons any more, not round here anyway.'

'You are evidently wrong,' said the king. We had reached Flower Street. December stuck his right arm out from my pocket and pointed in the direction of the market. 'See? There's one just there!'

I looked towards the market. Sure enough, in the midst of the cars that were, as usual, queuing to get into Lady Street, there was an enormous, terrible dragon, about as long as a bus and bright blue. Its body was covered in little round, straw-like tubes which puffed exhaust fumes. His nostrils breathed fire with such ferocity and such a noise that it was as if a helicopter were flying over our heads. Nobody seemed at all concerned. The dragon moved along slowly with the cars; turned right at the corner, and disappeared behind the houses.

'Incredible,' I said, and stood for several minutes staring at where the dragon had been, completely flabbergasted. 'What's a dragon doing here?'

'He's attacking people on their way to the office,' replied the king. 'He doesn't want them to go so he's trying to stop them.'

'He's never attacked me,' I said.

'Really?' the king asked. 'Have you never, on the way into work, felt something holding you back? As if something was holding on to you and stopping you from going on? And have you never felt as though there was something squeezing you round your chest?'

'Well, yes, of course I have,' I replied. 'But I thought that was just because I didn't want to go to the office, or because I was afraid of my boss, or that I wouldn't be able to do my work.'

'That was the dragon. He was pulling you back, or he was grabbing you from behind and squeezing you tight around your chest.'

'But I've never seen him. And why didn't he attack me today?'

'Because you're not going to the office today.'

'Aha!'

We walked on a little further, till we reached a café and went in. The king sat in my pocket looking out the whole time. I had given up trying to make him hide or push him back in. When the waitress came over to us I was sure she would say, 'My goodness! You have the funniest little king in your jacket pocket!' But she only asked me what I wanted to order.

'A cappuccino, please,' I answered. 'And you don't have any jelly bears, by any chance?'

'I think so,' she replied. 'For children. Yes, I think we do.'

She brought my coffee and a little bag of jelly bears. I took one out for the king.

'Thank you very much,' he said.

I sprinkled some sugar into my cappuccino and watched how the sugar formed a little island in the foam before sinking.

'It's sad to go to the office every day and not see the things you see,' I said. 'And to keep having to fight the dragon without knowing that that's what it is.'

'Yes,' said the king, happily biting into his jelly bear. 'Can I have the rest of the jelly bears in the bag too?'

'I wish I were like you,' I said.

'You can't be like me,' said the king. 'But you were once. When you were little, I mean.'

'But now I'm big, and you're getting smaller and smaller,' I said.

'That is wonderful,' said the king. 'For me, I mean.'

'Yes, for you . . .'

'Well anyway, I am your little king,' he said, 'and I live with you. I'm only here because you wished it.'

I stirred my coffee.

'That's good, isn't it?'

'Yes, it certainly is,' I said.

One beautiful summer evening King December and I went out on to the balcony. We lay on our backs and looked up at the stars. Well, to be exact, I lay on my back on the ground. The king lay on my stomach between the fifth and sixth shirt buttons from the top, and I could feel his light little body rising and falling with my breath.

'What do you feel when you look at the stars?' he asked.

'I feel small and unimportant,' I replied. 'I feel as small as you are; smaller, even. And the earth feels gigantic and I am just a tiny speck.'

'Down here you're so big, and yet the minute you look at the stars way up there you feel tiny?'

'Yes,' I said. 'Like a little wheel that no one misses when it rolls off into a dark corner.'

'Do you know what I feel?' said the king. 'I feel enormous. I grow as big as the universe; but not like a balloon you blow up that will eventually burst. It feels completely natural and gentle. I don't feel stretched or anything like that. It's like I'm the air. In the end, I'm not just a part of a whole. I *am* the whole, and the

stars are part of *me*. Can you imagine what it feels like?'

I was silent for a moment. And then I answered, 'No.'

'That doesn't surprise me,' he said. 'If you could, then you would feel it too, and you would have realised long ago how good it feels.' Huffing and puffing, he rolled himself over on to his tummy and looked up into my face. 'So, which is the truth then? Are you as big as you look, or as small as you feel?'

'I don't know,' I answered, and looked up at the sky.

King December looked at me and said, 'Why do you feel small when you look at something big?'

I said nothing.

'If I feel that I am everything, and you feel that you are only a small part,' he continued, 'then you must be a part of me. But I'm not a part of you.'

Still I said nothing.

'Odd, isn't it?' said the king.

'Yes, it's odd.'

'Do you miss me, then?' he asked.

'Yes,' I said. 'I think there are quite a few people who feel the lack of a little king, without even knowing it.'

The king had lain his head to one side, his ear to my stomach.

'You're lucky that I'm still as big as your little finger, and you can still see me. One day I'll be so small you won't be able to see me any more. If we hadn't met until then, it would have been too late.'

'For me,' I said.

'For you,' said the king. He sat up, right on my belly button, reclining in its hollow as if he were in a basket chair. 'Shall we play a game? Shall we pretend something?'

'What?'

'Have you ever imagined that you were immortal?'

'No.' I lifted my head to look at him. 'What does it feel like?'

'Good question,' replied the king, squirming with pleasure in my belly button.

'Yes,' I said. 'And what's the answer?'

'A very good question,' he said again.

'And . . . ?'

'Damn good.'

'But the answer?' I insisted, beginning to lose patience.

'You're making progress. At first you had no imagination, but now you ask such good questions.'

'Answer me!' I cried.

'Do you think I know everything?' he shouted all of a sudden. He had sprung up, and stood on one of my shirt buttons as if it were a podium, waving his sceptre about in the air. 'An answer to every question, is that what you want? Is it early? Or is it late? Ask his Majesty! Think for yourself! Or did you invent me simply to do all your thinking for you, so you would never have to bother your pretty little head ever again?'

'OK, OK,' I said. 'I'll imagine then.'

Puffing loudly, the king made himself comfortable again.

'Well, I think,' I said, 'it probably all began with a good fairy.'

'A good fairy? Well, that remains to be seen,' he butted in grumpily.

'One day a fairy appeared by the side of my bed, leaned over me, letting her long silver hair brush my face, and said:

'Hourdigourdischlompidomp
Roumpisoumpinoudelpomp
Ridelradellendencort
Oh, how the days are short!
Time – let's fritter it away . . .
You'll never see your dying day.'

'Well?' asked the king. 'Are you afraid or happy?'

'First of all, I have to work out if it's true or not,' I replied. 'Why should I believe the fairy?'

'You could try to kill yourself,' he suggested.

'How horrible!' I cried. 'Kill myself? Just when I've become immortal! And you might survive a suicide attempt, and then, just think . . . immortal and stuck in a wheelchair . . .'

'Breathe more slowly!' shouted King December. 'I'm beginning to feel seasick down here.'

'I'd probably get a letter from my pension fund,' I said. 'They'd write: "Dear sir, due to your immortality and the considerably heightened costs which we will consequently incur, we regret that we will have to increase your premiums. As they have remained unchanged for some time, we are sure you will understand our position.'

'What is a pension fund?' asked the king.

'Each month, for your whole life, you pay money into a fund, so that when you are old you get money back every month,' I said. 'That way, you don't need to worry about getting old.'

'Are you afraid of getting old?'

'Of getting old? No, not really,' I replied. 'But I am afraid of what comes after that.'

'And you can't insure against that?'

'No,' I said.

'I'm not afraid,' said the king. 'And yet I have no pension fund. The smaller I get, the more I can lie on the balcony and stare at the stars and imagine things.' He looked me straight in the eye. 'You wanted to imagine what it felt like to be immortal. But so far all you've done is talk about your funny little fairy and your pension fund.'

'All you do is grouse at me,' I said, and looked up into the sky again.

The king laid his head back, looked up too and said: 'I bet you don't have a favourite star, either.'

'No,' I said. 'I don't.'

'Then choose one, and give it a name!' said King December.

I stared up at the sky for a long time, looking for a particularly fine star. I found one, shining very faintly, right next to the Plough, and pointed it out to the king, saying: 'It's called Stanley.'

'Normally stars are called Alpha Centauri. Or Betelgeuse,' he said. 'I think it's nice that yours is called Stanley.'

'I had a friend called that once,' I said. 'He died a long time ago.'

'And when you die, you become a star,' the king said.

'Well, if that's true, and I'm immortal, then all my friends will be stars one day, except me. And after they die, on clear nights I'd be able to look up at them. And the only thing I'd know for sure would be that I'd never know what they know.'

The king was staring quietly to the right of the Plough, when suddenly he became very excited. He leaped up and started walking up and down my tummy so fast that he was tickling me and it was all I could do to stop myself laughing.

'Remember how I said I couldn't remember how we come

into the world? A king and a queen had to do something, but I didn't know what any more? That's what I said, isn't it? And that one morning we just woke up, big, like you, lying in bed, and from then on, all our lives we just got smaller and smaller. I told you, didn't I?'

'Yes, that's what you told me.'

'Well, I've remembered again, what it is that the king and queen have to do,' he said.

'What?' I asked.

'They have to put their arms round each other . . .'

'Well, I know that,' I said.

'They have to put their arms round each other on a balcony, like this one, hug each other really tight, then close their eyes and jump off.'

'Jump off?'

'They have to jump off the balcony. If they are holding on to each other tight enough and have their eyes closed tight enough, when they hit the ground it's like a trampoline and they spring up into the sky. And then they catch a star and lay it in a bed. And in the morning when it wakes up, it's one of us.'

'Are you sure?'

'Absolutely,' he said.

'And have you done this?' I asked.

'Of course.'

'You weren't frightened?'

'Yes, but my queen was holding on to me very tightly.'

'So, if what you say is true, every person, at one time or another, will be chosen and will wake up a little king . . . And then they'll get smaller and smaller until you can't see them any more?'

'Well, yes.'

'Oh – that's very sad for me.'

'Why?'

'Because I'm immortal.'

'You're not immortal at all,' replied King December. 'We were just pretending.'

'True! I'd completely forgotten.' I lifted my head again to look at the king, who had walked up from my stomach to my chest, then along my neck, and was now struggling to clamber up on to my face. As he reached my chin, I stuttered: 'Are you really . . .'

'Careful! Speak slowly!' cried the king nervously. 'Or I might fall in your mouth and you'll swallow me!'

'Are you really immortal?' I asked.

'What makes you think that?'

'What does the end of your life mean for you?' I asked. 'I mean, where does the getting smaller stop? Your father is so small that you can't see him any more, but does that mean he's not there? Maybe he's here, walking about beside us, and your grandmother too, and your grandfather. They're tiny, like specks of dust, and you can't crush them because they slip through the finest chink in the sole of your shoe. If that's the case, then maybe you just keep on getting smaller, and life has no end.'

As I was talking, the king wobbled about, like a walking stick you're trying to balance upright on your hand. He was staring deep into my open mouth.

'How should I know?' he said.

I n winter, when I get home from work in the evening, I throw
three or four logs into my old green enamel stove and light
it. And once the room has warmed up, I settle myself into my old
armchair by the bookshelves and look through the window at the
snow falling in fat, wet flakes, the size of little kings' heads.

Sometimes it's very quiet, and at other times I can hear voices
through the walls because they're so thin. Thin? Well, I don't
know exactly how thick the walls really are. And are the voices
really coming from the apartment next door? Or from the wall
itself, which isn't really so thin, but tremendously thick, thick
enough to hold the entire universe of the little King December.

At first, I thought of knocking a hole in the wall – taking a
pickaxe and breaking through to see what's behind it. But then I
thought I might find myself standing in a strange dining room,
covered in dust, with a bewildered family looking up from their
dinner to stare at me. 'I'm terribly sorry,' I'd mumble, embarrassed.
'I was just looking for the little king.'

Once King December scolded me: 'Why do you feel the need

to look behind walls instead of imagining what might be inside them? Why don't you just sit down, close your eyes and invent your own world? When you were little you did, even with your eyes open. Have you forgotten how to? How could you forget?'

On one particular quiet winter's evening, I had no sooner sat down than the king came out from behind my bookcase.

He didn't come over to me right away, however. First he went over to the other side of the room where I'd left a couple of old toy cars lying around. I've had them since I was thirteen, and have never seen any reason to throw them away. He opened the door of an old Mercedes truck and climbed in. It's a blue truck, with red bumpers and quite a short flatbed behind. There are two flashing yellow lights on the roof and, attached to the back by a large red hook, an odd sort of trailer. Completely flat, with twelve wheels, it's designed for transporting railway carriages if they need to be taken somewhere and there's no railway. At that time it was empty.

The king threw a half-eaten jelly bear into the back of the truck. And because he was still a little bit too big, and too fat, he had to do all sorts of contortions to squeeze into the cabin, puffing and moaning and swearing, grumbling that he couldn't wait for the day when he's tiny enough to fit in comfortably. Then he started the truck, which rumbled over the floor to my chair, the motor purring softly. When he was about level with my foot he rolled down the window, leaned out and shouted: 'Hey! We've got things to do today, you know!'

'What?' I asked.

'We've got to deliver a picture to the great collector.'

'The great collector?'

'You don't know the great collector?'

'No,' I said. 'I've never heard of him.'

'The great collector is very rich and he lives just by the stove,' said the king. 'Nobody owns as many paintings as he does.'

'So why are you delivering another one to him?' I asked.

'Well, kings have to sell a picture every so often in order to survive.'

'And what do you get for your picture?'

'Jelly bears,' said the king. 'I only have the one in the truck left. But shall we have a game of something first, before we go?'

The king and I play a game of something nearly every day – pick-up-sticks, for example: he lugs the sticks about like great timbers. Or chess! King December always plays as his own king. When he is white and has made his move, he has to dash back to the White King's square and wait until I make my move. When he is checkmated, he falls theatrically to the ground and cries: 'Thy fierce hand hath with the king's blood stain'd the king's own land.'

When he wins, he rushes up to my king, his arms outstretched, and knocks it over with a cry: 'Here, thou incestuous, murderous, damned Dane, Drink of this potion! . . .'

One day I said to him: 'I thought you forgot everything when you got smaller and older. Everything except Shakespeare, I take it?'

'Richard II! And Claudius, King of Denmark,' cried the king. 'Such colleagues are not easily forgotten!'

On this particular day, the king said he needed some exercise, so I fished out the Tipp-Kick – a small table-football game where the players have movable legs and a button on top of their head which you press to make them kick the ball. The king, of course, doesn't need a button. He takes off his heavy red velvet coat and dribbles up and down the green playing field in his underwear, and when he scores a goal he kisses his little metallic team-mates and falls wheezing to the ground. He always gets out of breath very quickly when he plays football, because he's so fat.

'That's not fair!' I cry. 'You can run, but my players can't!'

'Those stiff little metal men! Well, I'm totally exhausted, and they aren't!'

'Do you still have to deliver your picture?' I asked. 'Where is it? You don't seem to have a picture with you.'

'I still have to draw it,' he replied. 'Can you give me some paper and colouring pencils?'

I went to my desk and took out some paper and a box of pencils.

'It's all too big,' he says. 'You'll have to cut the paper so it fits on to the back of the truck. And the colouring pencils are like tree-trunks. Don't you have any little pencil stubs? I can't draw with tree-trunks.'

I went back to my desk and rooted about in the drawer amongst old batteries, tubes of glue, bits of string and broken

remote controls, until I found some scissors and a tiny end of a
light-green colouring pencil. I cut the paper into a piece that was
just a little bit longer than the truck trailer, but exactly the right
width. I gave the pencil stub to the king, who said: 'Light green is
no good. I wanted to draw a seven-pointed crown – light green is
simply the wrong colour.'

'This is the only one I have that's small enough for you,' I
replied. 'All the others are too big, and I don't need to go looking
in that drawer for a pencil sharpener – I know I won't find one.'

The king was already deep in thought and mumbling to
himself: 'Well, it will have to do. I'll just say that it's deliberate.

Other painters have their blue periods – he'll be pleased to have a pale-green crown drawing of mine.'

He lifted the pencil with both arms and stood on the paper. He went up and down with small steps and slowly and shakily drew a pale-green crown with seven points.

'Do you like it?' he asked.

'It's beautiful,' I said. 'I've never understood why crowns have to be gold anyway.'

'This one's made of oxidised copper,' King December said. 'It belongs to End-of-November, King of the Gutters. Will you help me put it on to the trailer?'

He took hold of one end of the painting with both hands and I took the other end between my thumb and forefinger and we carefully laid it on our truck.

Then he said: 'Get in – we're off!'

'How am I supposed to get into this tiny truck?' I asked.

'Oh, yes – well, sit down in your chair, close your eyes and just imagine that you're getting in. That'll do it.'

I did as he said, sat in my chair, closed my eyes and soon felt as small as King December – not as fat, thank goodness, but as small. The king climbed back into the driver's seat and said again: 'Get in!'

He opened the passenger door and I climbed in. 'Where exactly does he live again, the great collector?'

'Right beside the stove – behind the skirting board,' said the king, starting the engine. 'There's a small hole between the skirting board and the wall, and he lives behind there.'

'Have you been to his place before?' I asked.

The king drove along the parquet boards to avoid the cracks, but each time we had to go over one, the whole truck shook and our heads banged against the roof. Every time this happened his crown nearly fell off and he had to fix it back on his head.

'Of course I've been there before – many times,' he said. 'I deliver a picture to him almost every month.'

We drove round a table leg which seemed like a giant tree-trunk.

'What's it like, his place?'

'There are lots of rooms,' he replied 'Big ones, little ones – some are as huge as a sports hall, others are smaller than a food cupboard. Sometimes you have to climb a narrow spiral staircase to get to a room, then there'll be a set of steps bigger than a castle's. There are pictures hanging on every wall.'

'Do they all belong to the great collector?' I asked. 'Does he live alone there?'

We had turned left at the table leg and were now steering straight towards the oven.

'He lives all alone,' said the king. 'And all the paintings belong to him.' The truck bounced over a particularly deep crack and I looked anxiously out of the back window because I was worried we might have lost the picture. But it was still there, lying on the trailer, and the nibbled jelly bear was still in the back of the truck

'You see,' said King December. 'I think you have to imagine the great collector's apartment like the inside of a head. All our life, we observe the world and collect millions of pictures in our heads. We look at some of them nearly every day, but some are hanging in distant rooms and we only see them if we search long and hard, or come across them by accident. But they are there, even if we don't remember them any more – they are always in our head.'

'You sit in your chair . . . or you go for a walk. And see pictures you didn't even know were in your head.'

'Perhaps,' said the king. We reached the stove. He put the brakes on, switched the engine off and said, 'We need to unload the truck.'

We got out, lifted the picture off the trailer and carried it to the hole in the skirting board where the great collector lives.

The king shouted loudly into the hole. 'Picture collector! Picture collector, are you there?'

There was no reply. The king shouted again, listened for a moment and then said: 'He's probably somewhere in the house where he can't hear us. Sometimes all he does all day is wander through his rooms looking at his pictures. We'll leave the picture there by the skirting board and go. He'll fetch it as soon as he notices it's there, and then he'll leave my jelly bear in its place so I can come and collect it. We've often done that.'

The king had taken off his velvet coat, but nevertheless the unloading had put him into a sweat: it was very hot by the stove. We went back the way we came, and parked right by my armchair. As we got out, I said: 'Do you think the picture collector is a happy man?'

'Can you imagine that anyone who gets a picture of the Gutter King End-of-November's pale-green crown in return for a jelly bear can be an unhappy man?'

And he took the half-eaten bear from the back of the truck and went back to his crack in the wall behind the bookshelf, into which he always disappears. When he was gone, I opened my eyes as I sat there in my chair. Next to my right foot stood the little truck, and when I looked across the room I saw that next to the old stove, just by the skirting board where we had left the picture, there lay a red jelly bear.

First published by Verlag Antje Kunstmann GmbH, München 1993
under the title *Der kleine König Dezember* by Axel Hacke,
with illustrations by Michael Sowa

© Verlag Antje Kunstmann, Munich, 1993
This translation copyright © 2002 by Rosemary Davidson

Published by Bloomsbury, New York and London
Distributed to the trade by Holtzbrinck Publishers

Cataloguing-in-Publication Data is available from the Library of Congress

ISBN 1-58234-246-6

First US edition 2002

10 9 8 7 6 5 4 3 2 1

Typeset by Palimpsest Book Production Limited, Polmont, Stirlingshire
Printed and bound in Germany by Druckerei Uhl, Radolfzell